♡ Get Well, Eva ♡

Read more
OWL DIARIES books!

OWL DIARIES

♡ Get Well, Eva ♡

Rebecca Elliott

BRANCHES

SCHOLASTIC INC.

For all the amazing nurses
and everything they do for us.—R.E.

Special thanks to Ed Myer for
his contributions to this book.

Copyright © 2022 by Rebecca Elliott

All rights reserved. Published by Scholastic Inc., *Publishers
since 1920.* SCHOLASTIC, BRANCHES, and associated logos are
trademarks and/or registered trademarks of Scholastic Inc.

The publisher does not have any control over and does not assume any
responsibility for author or third-party websites or their content.

No part of this publication may be reproduced, stored in a retrieval system, or transmitted
in any form or by any means, electronic, mechanical, photocopying, recording, or otherwise,
without written permission of the publisher. For information regarding permission, write to
Scholastic Inc., Attention: Permissions Department, 557 Broadway, New York, NY 10012.

This book is a work of fiction. Names, characters, places, and incidents are either the
product of the author's imagination or are used fictitiously, and any resemblance to actual
persons, living or dead, business establishments, events, or locales is entirely coincidental.

Library of Congress Cataloging-in-Publication Data
Names: Elliott, Rebecca, author, illustrator. | Elliott, Rebecca. Owl diaries ; 16.
Title: Get well, Eva / Rebecca Elliott.
Description: First edition. | New York : Branches/Scholastic Inc., 2022. |
Series: Owl diaries ; 16 |
Summary: When Eva hurts her wing, she visits the hospital and meets a
new friend, Rocco, who has a broken leg—but wearing a sling for a week
prevents her from writing in her diary, and she turns to her
friends and family in order to keep it up-to-date.
Identifiers: LCCN 2021013034 | ISBN 9781338745405 (paperback) |
ISBN 9781338745412 (library binding)
Subjects: LCSH: Owls—Juvenile fiction. | Wounds and injuries—Juvenile
fiction. | Friendship—Juvenile fiction. | Diaries—Juvenile fiction. |
CYAC: Owls—Fiction. | Wounds and injuries—Fiction. |
Friendship—Fiction. | Diaries—Fiction. | LCGFT: Diary fiction.
Classification: LCC PZ7.E45812 Ge 2022 | DDC [Fic]—dc23
LC record available at https://lccn.loc.gov/2021013034

10 9 8 7 6 5 4 3 2 1   22 23 24 25 26

Printed in China   62
First edition, March 2022

Edited by Rachel Matson
Book design by Marissa Asuncion

♡ Table of Contents ♡

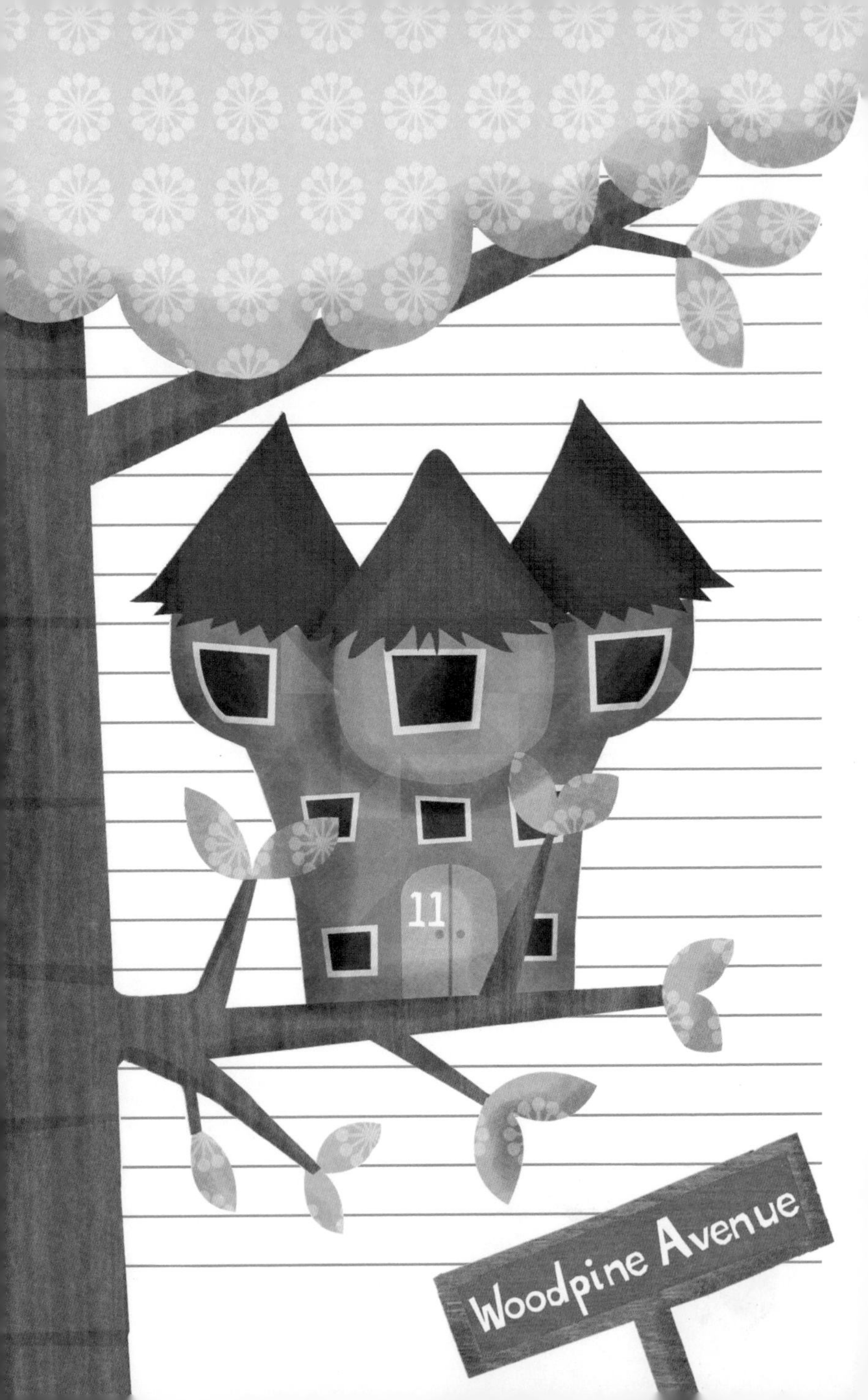
11
Woodpine Avenue

1

♡ Carnival Is Coming! ♡

Sunday

Hi Diary,

Yes, it's me, your favorite owl, Eva Wingdale! Today I heard some **FLAPERRIFIC** news. Treetopolis is holding its SUMMER CARNIVAL on Friday! There will be lots of games to play and fun food to eat. I can't wait!

But more about that later . . .

I love:

Writing in
my diary

Having fun with
my friends

Carnival games

Eating carnival
food

Jumping in
bouncy houses

Getting my face
painted

The word <u>bobbing</u>

Winning prizes

<u>I DO NOT love:</u>

Humphrey reading my diary

<u>Being away from my friends</u>

<u>Difficult carnival games</u>

<u>Getting cotton candy stuck in my feathers</u>

Waiting in long lines

When it's time to take off the face paint

The word <u>damp</u>

Not winning prizes

This is my **OWLMAZING** family at the carnival last year.

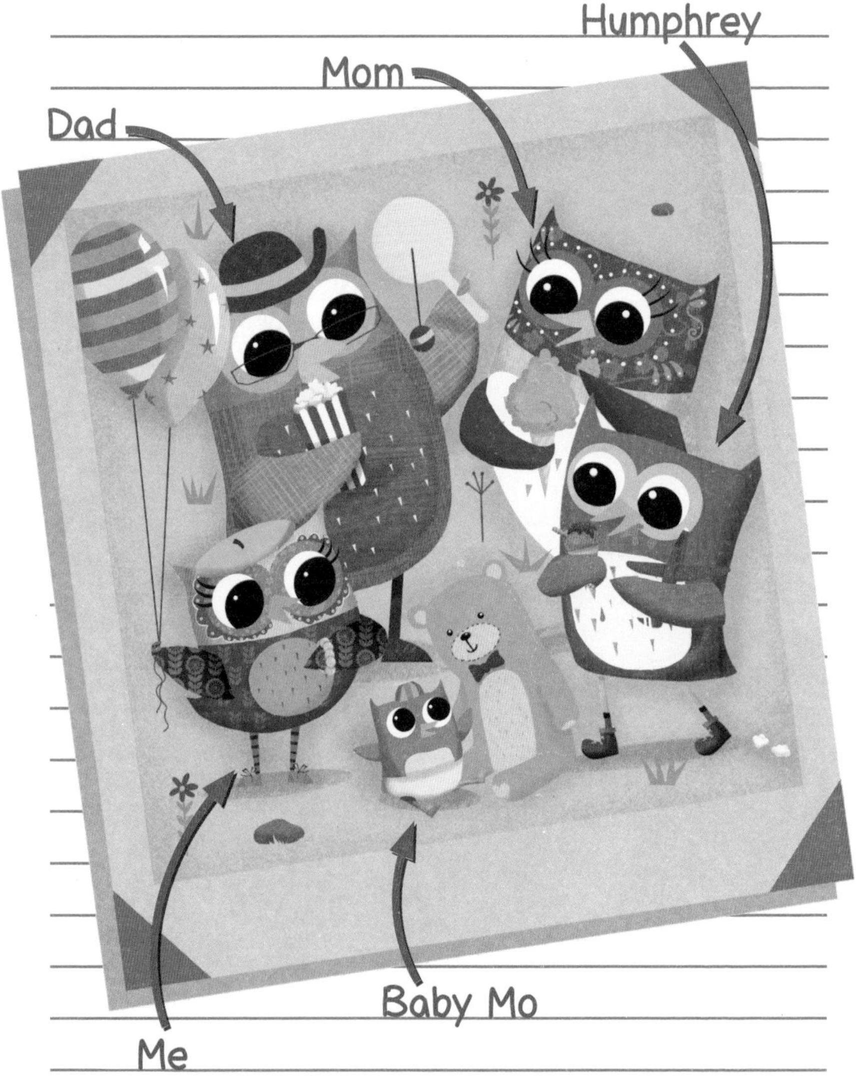
Humphrey
Mom
Dad
Baby Mo
Me

And these are my cute pets! Baxter is a bat, and Acorn is a flying squirrel.

Being an owl is **FLAPPY-FABULOUS**.

Our BIG eyes can see in the dark.

Our heads can turn all the way around to look behind us.

Our beaks help us HOOT loudly.

Our wings are super strong so we can fly really fast!

I live at number 11 Woodpine Avenue in Treetopolis. My **BFF** (Best Feathery Friend), Lucy Beakman, lives right next door.

We both go to Treetop Owlementary School with our other friends. Here is our class photo.

Zara
Hailey
Sue
Kiera
Carlos
Zac

Jacob Macy
George
Me
Lilly
Lucy
Mrs. Featherbottom

I can't wait to go to school tomorrow. I bet we'll be doing lots of exciting carnival stuff all week long!

♡ Let the Games Begin! ♡

Monday

This evening, Mrs. Featherbottom told the class that we are going to run our very own game at the carnival on Friday! We just needed to decide what game to make.

There were some really good ideas.

What about a beanbag toss?

Or how about guessing the weight of my pet snail, Flash?

Or a spinning prize-wheel game?

SPIN the WHEEL

In the end, we decided to go with Lucy's idea! We all got to work on making a big spinning wheel.

Great! And maybe if they land on red, they get to choose an extra-special prize?
I love it!
But what will the extra-special prizes be?
I know! We could make some!
That's a great idea!

We flew around the forest collecting
things we could use to make prizes.

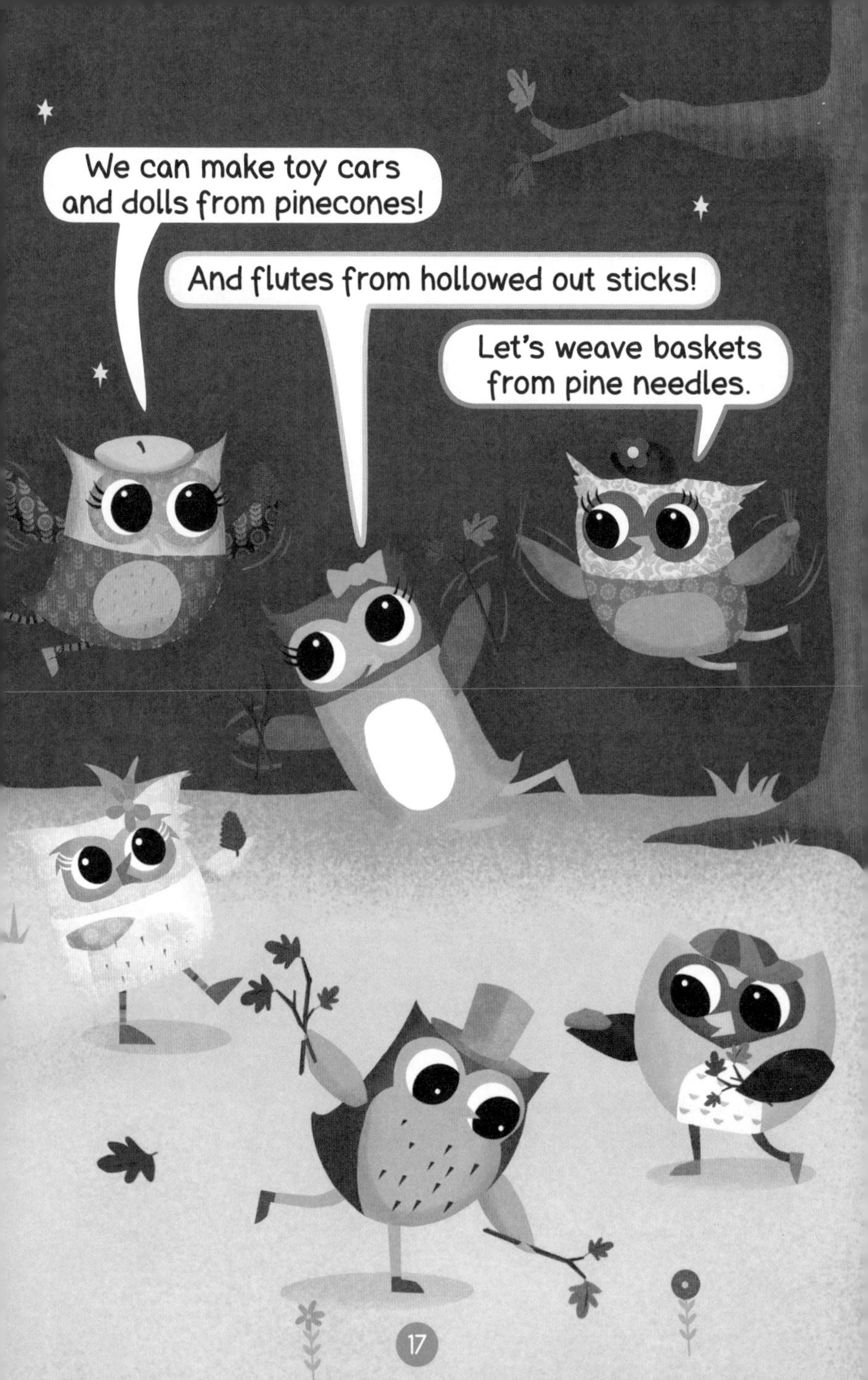
We can make toy cars and dolls from pinecones!
And flutes from hollowed out sticks!
Let's weave baskets from pine needles.

Back in the classroom, we got to work making our prizes. Then Mrs. Featherbottom said something else exciting.

There will also be a competition on Friday — for who can design the best carnival hat. The mayor will decide who wins!

Oh, how exciting! Let's enter the contest!

Definitely. Our hats are going to be the best!

Well, my mom's a fashion designer. So mine will probably be the best. But good luck.

Lucy and I got to work on our hat designs. Do you like them, Diary?

My design

Lucy's design

But back at my house, we didn't do too much hat making. Mom was making loads of blueberry jam to give out as prizes at Grandpa and Granny's carnival game. We helped her instead. Then we had a blueberry fight!

Jam making was **WINGTASTIC** fun. But now I think I <u>might</u> need to get cleaned up and go to bed!

Diary Takeover!

Tuesday

Hello, Eva's diary! This is Lucy. I know it's strange for me to be writing in here, but Eva asked me to. Let me explain what happened . . .

At school tonight, we were all having such a great time playing wingball. Eva swooped down to make an **OWLMAZING** save.

But then . . . DISASTER!!!

She hit her wing on a tree branch and went spiraling to the ground!

Luckily, she landed in a soft pile of leaves. But she hurt her wing really badly.

So badly, in fact, that she can't write in her diary! That's why she asked me to write in here instead.

I kept Eva company at home while she rested her wing.

How's your wing feeling, Eva?

It doesn't hurt too much, but I can't really move it!

I think we should take you to the hospital. The doctor should check your wing.

I agree, Eva. I'll pack some things for you in case you need to stay a whole day.

Good luck, Eva! And get well soon, because I miss you already!

Hi, Eva's diary. This is Humphrey, Eva's awesome brother! I'm at the hospital with Eva at the moment. She told me I can write in here so long as I DO NOT look through the rest of her diary. I _probably_ won't do that . . .

Humphrey!

What?! I only had a quick look.

The doctors are putting a **WINGSLING** on Eva now. It has to stay on until Saturday so her wing heals.

Eva has to stay in the hospital until tomorrow. Then she gets a **WINGCHAIR** to use. It's so unfair. I wish I could try using one!

See you tomorrow, Sis. Hope your wing gets better soon.

Aw, thanks, Humphrey.

Just because I don't want to do all the chores on my own for too long!

Truth is, Eva is being pretty brave about the whole thing. I have to go home with my parents now. See you later, Eva's diary!

4

♡ Hospital Friends ♡

Wednesday

Hi, Diary! It's me again! My wing is feeling a lot better now that it's in this cool wingsling. I have to use my other wing to write, though, which is tricky! Sorry if my handwriting is a bit shaky!

I'm still in the hospital. But staying here has actually been quite fun!

They bring you lots of yummy food.

The nurses are all really sweet.

The wingchair is SO MUCH fun to fly around in!

You're really getting the hang of that chair, Eva!

There's a great playroom, too. And the BEST thing is — I made a new friend!

Rocco is from the next forest over. It's called Woodingsville. He was vacationing in Treetopolis with his family when he tripped over his suitcase and hurt his leg.

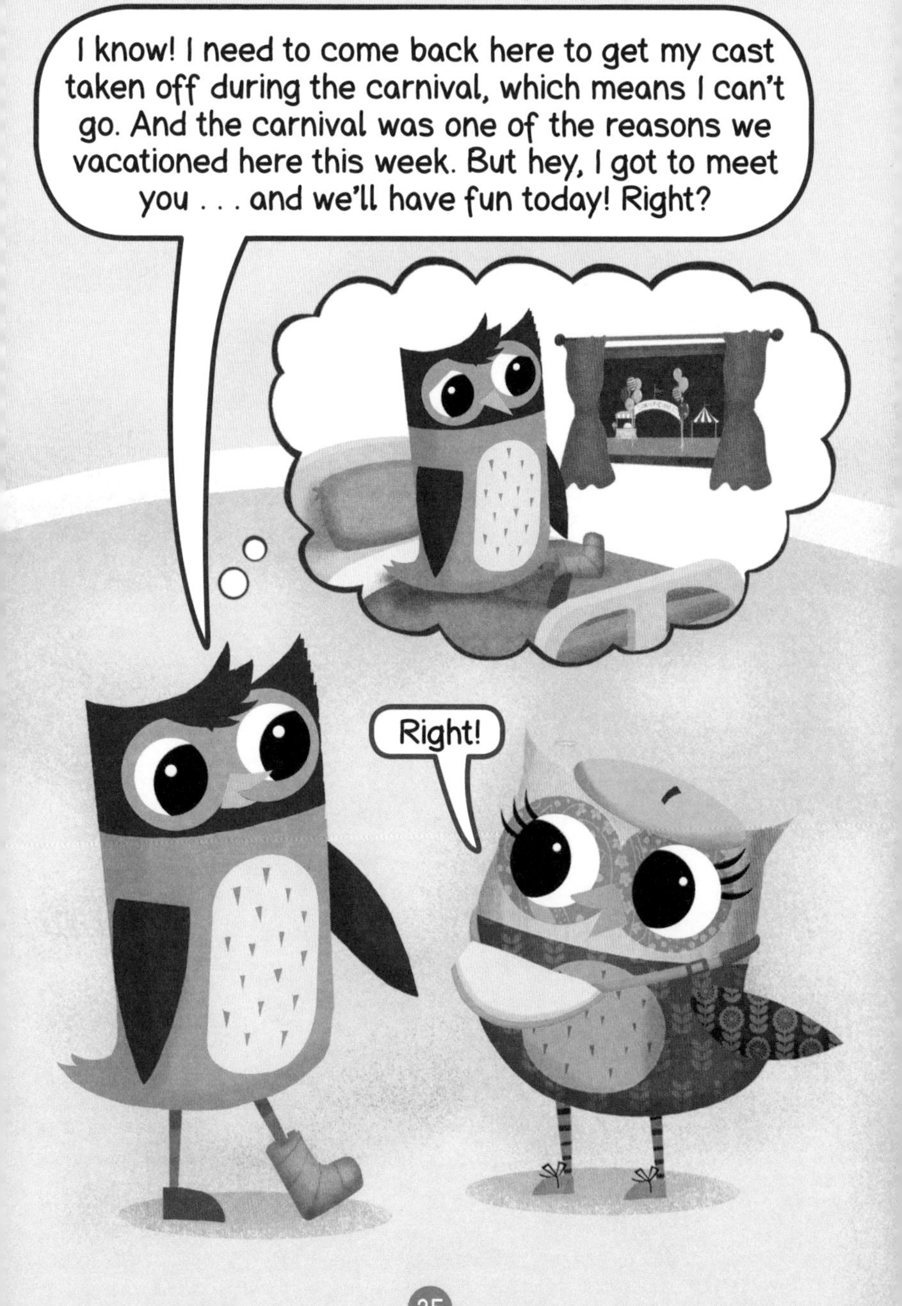
I know! I need to come back here to get my cast taken off during the carnival, which means I can't go. And the carnival was one of the reasons we vacationed here this week. But hey, I got to meet you . . . and we'll have fun today! Right?
Right!

Rocco and I talked for ages and had so much fun together.

We watched a great movie.

We made balloons out of surgical gloves!

And we threw chocolate in the air and caught it in our beaks!

We even had some great wingchair races around the hospital garden!

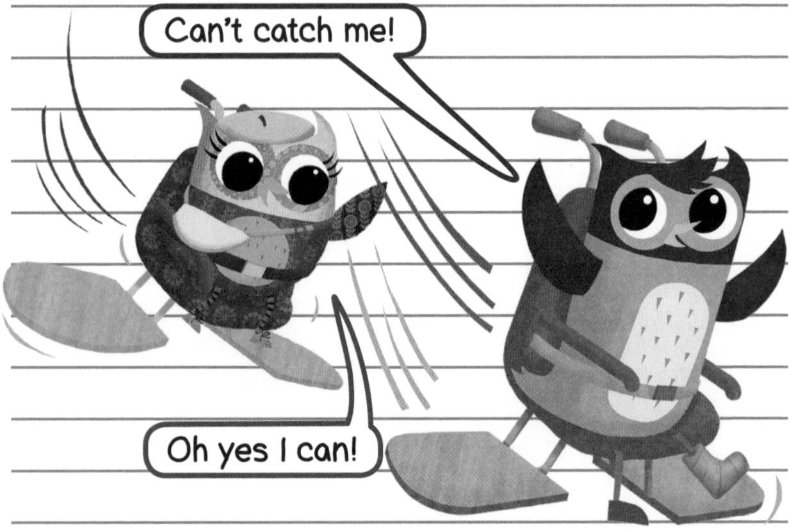
Can't catch me!
Oh yes I can!

Then it was time for our parents to pick us up. He signed my wingsling, and I signed his cast.

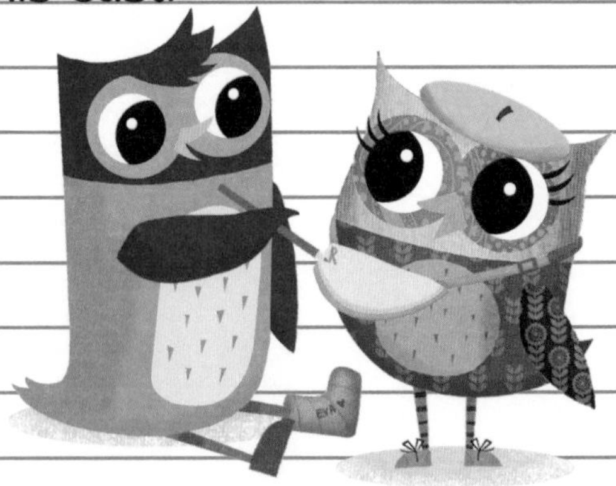

Then we swapped addresses.

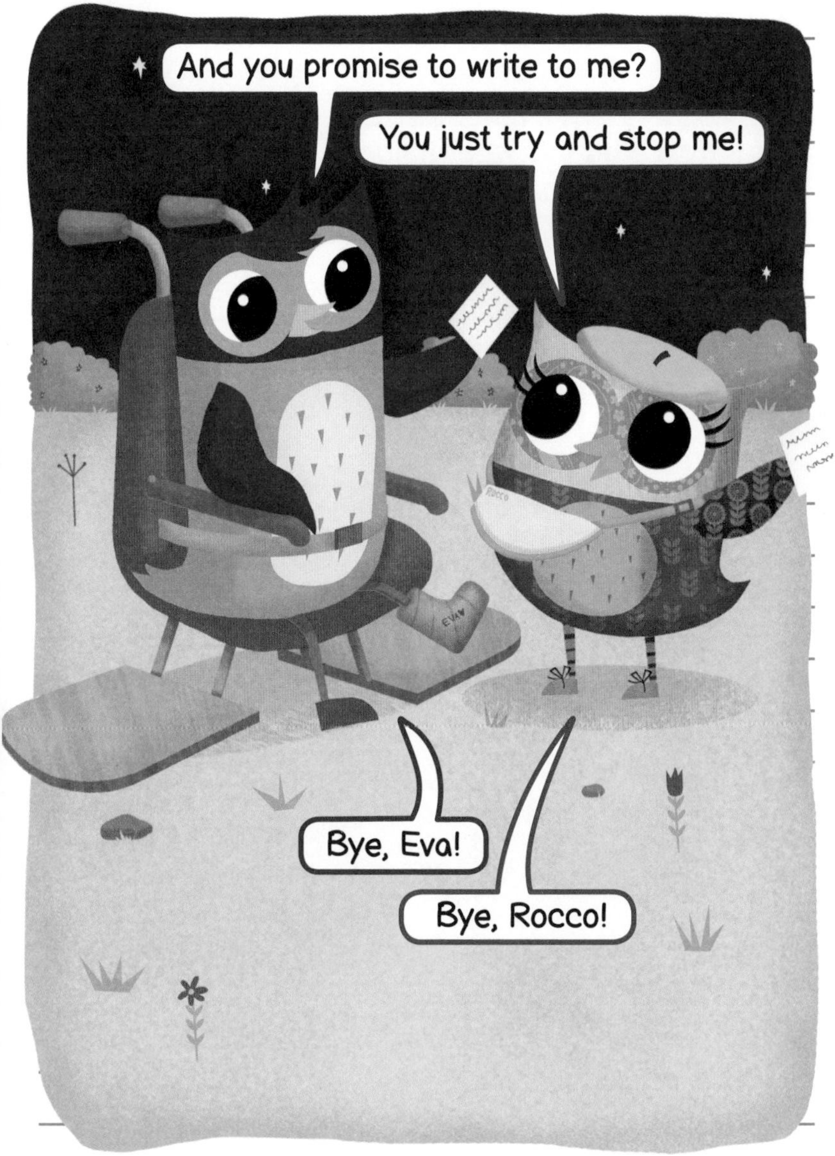
And you promise to write to me?
You just try and stop me!
Bye, Eva!
Bye, Rocco!

Back at home, Lucy came over before bedtime.

I told her about my new friend Rocco.

I'm sorry he can't come to the carnival. But at least you can — it's going to be great!

It really will be. But I wish I could have finished my hat for the competition.

Don't worry, we don't need silly hats to have fun! We're going to have the best time, Eva, you'll see.

I'm sure Lucy's right. But mostly, I just feel a bit sad that I might not get to see Rocco again.

5

♡ Spin the Wheel! ♡

Thursday

School was wonderful tonight, Diary. Everyone was excited to see me flying around in my wingchair.

Wow! That's so fast, Eva!

42

And everyone signed my wingsling.

Then at recess, we hung out with Macy's little sister, Mia. She uses a wingchair all the time and showed me some great new tricks!

Look, Eva! If you do this, you can do a backflip!

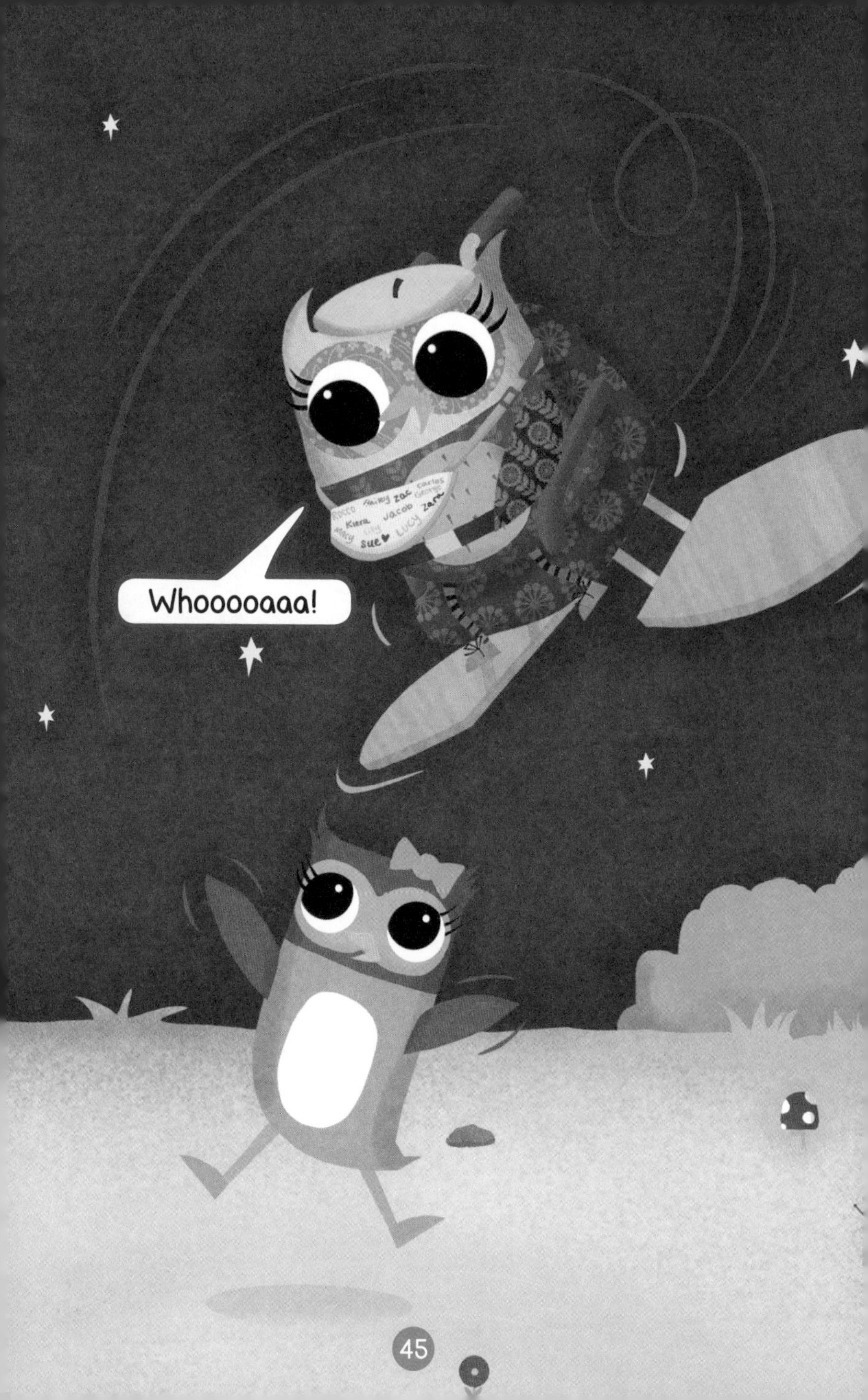
Whooooaaa!

After recess, the class worked on our carnival game. I tried to help paint a section. But I had to use my other wing, which meant everything was messier than I wanted. Nothing came out right.

    I did some quiet reading for the rest of the school night while my friends finished the wheel. I wished I could talk to Rocco. He can't use one of his legs right now, so he might understand how frustrated this makes me feel.

I was still feeling a bit sad about not being able to join in with making the spinning wheel when Lucy and Hailey flew over to me.

The wheel looked great. I gave it a spin, and it landed on a blue section.

49

This time I gave the wheel a BIG spin.

It landed on a red "Pick a Prize" section.

I didn't know what was going on. But then Lucy came back in the room with . . .

Oh, Diary. That was such a lovely thing my friends did for me. Look at this beautiful hat! It's EXACTLY like I had designed it. I'm still sad that Rocco can't come to the carnival tomorrow. But I am looking forward to wearing my hat! I'll try to have a good time and not worry about Rocco too much.

6

♥ Carnival Time! ♥

Friday

The carnival was **OWLMAZING**!!

SUMMER CARNIVAL

52

We took turns running our spinning wheel game. And we ate yummy carnival food and played some super fun games.

Here are some of the games we played:

The Beaver's
Beanbag Toss

The Farm Animals'
Duck Pond

The Bear's Balloon
Dart Throw

Granny Owlberta and
Grandpa Owlfred's
Ring the Bell

Finally, it was time for
the Carnival Hat Competition.

Everyone who made a carnival hat lined up.

Then the mayor decided . . .

The winner is Eva Wingdale!

I couldn't believe it!!

Thank you! I designed this hat, but my friends made it. They're winners, too!

The whole class flew up and took a bow while everyone cheered.

And that wasn't even the best thing . . .

The prize was loads of stuffed animals and cotton candy!

Well, I know exactly what I want to do with this prize! If it's okay with you, Mr. Swoopstone.

What, Eva?

I'd like to take these goodies to the hospital to share with all the owlets who couldn't be here today.

That's a great idea! Everyone, let's take the WHOLE carnival to the hospital!

Yay!

I was SO excited! We all flew to the hospital gardens with the prizes, food, and even some of the games. I couldn't wait to see the look on Rocco's face when he saw all of it!

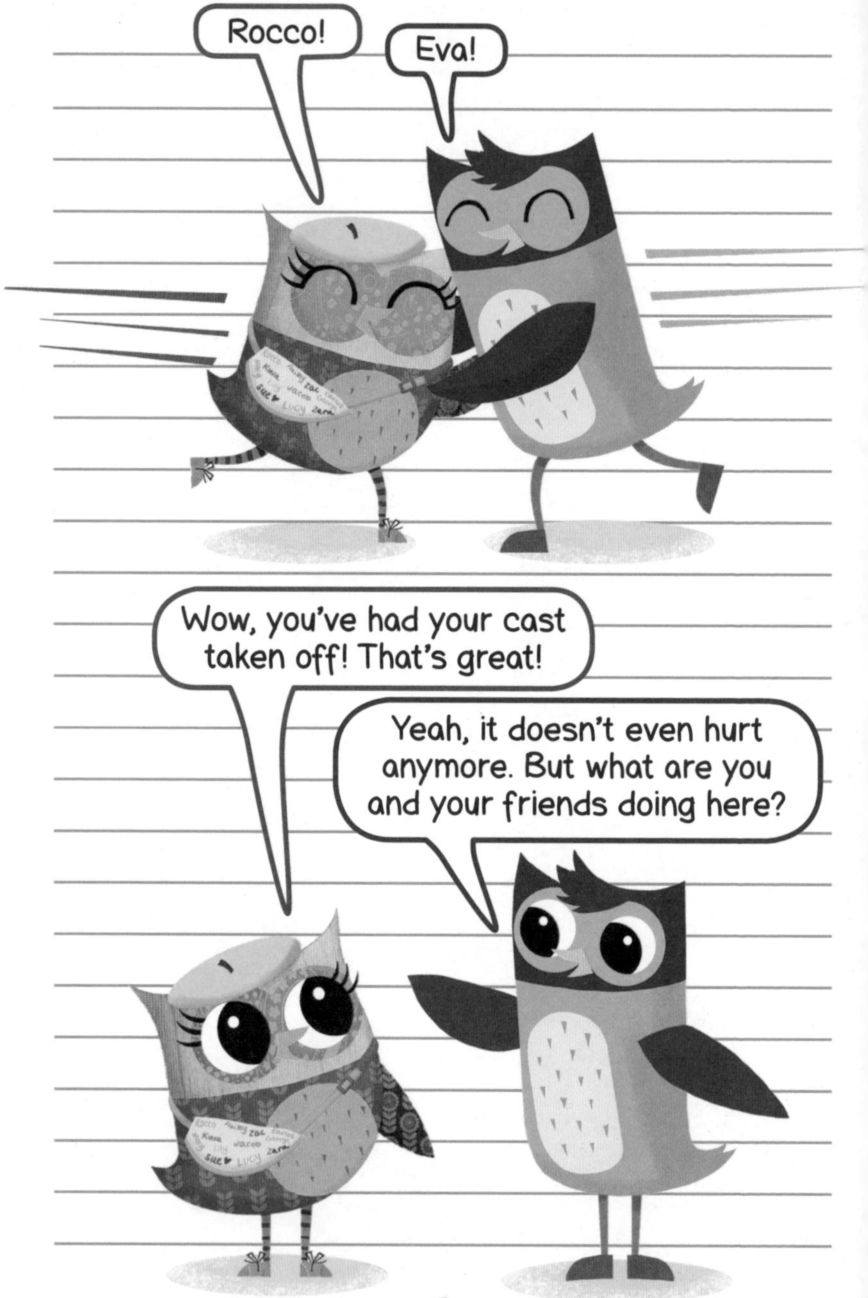
Rocco!
Eva!
Wow, you've had your cast taken off! That's great!
Yeah, it doesn't even hurt anymore. But what are you and your friends doing here?

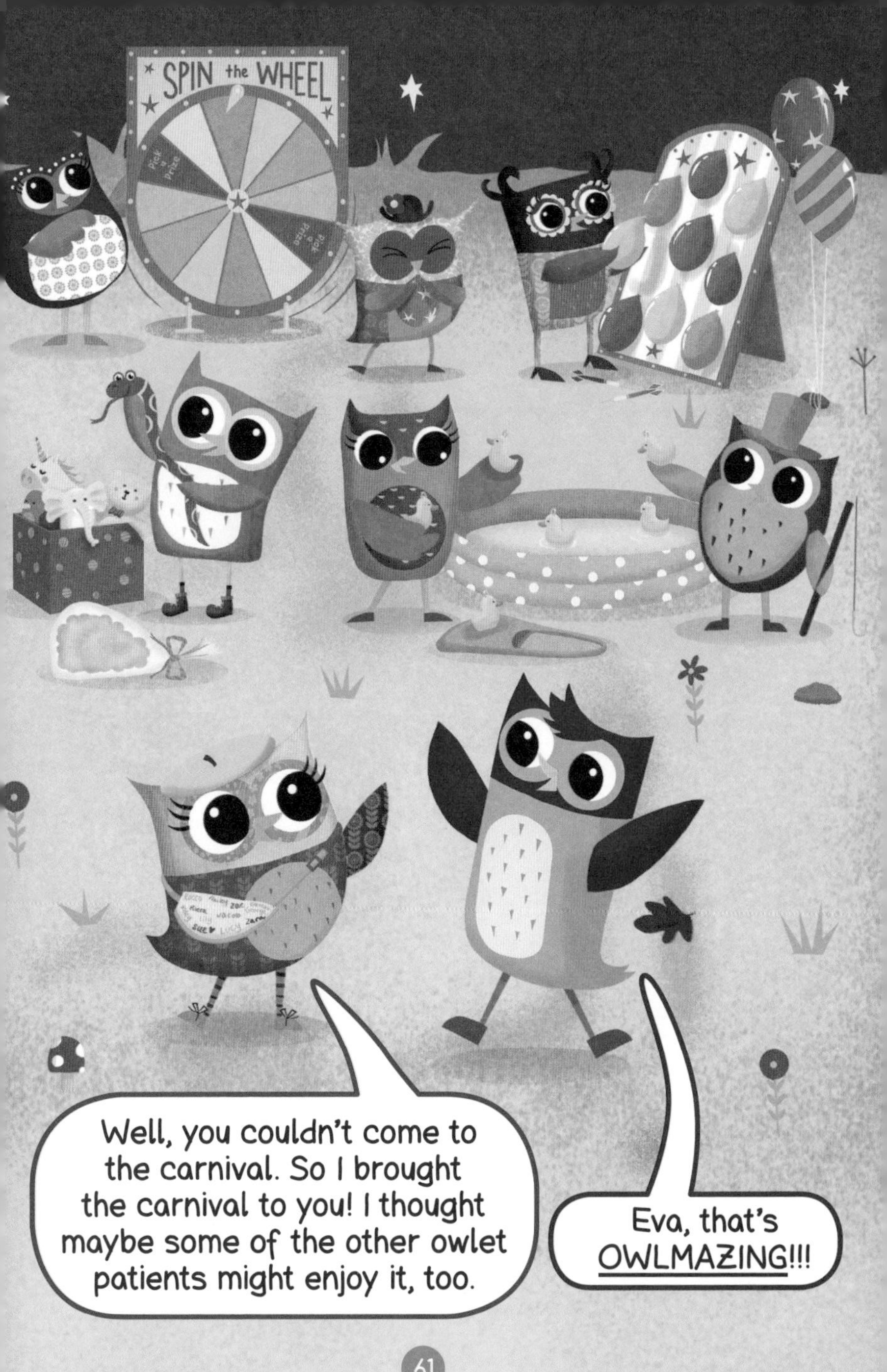
SPIN the WHEEL
Well, you couldn't come to the carnival. So I brought the carnival to you! I thought maybe some of the other owlet patients might enjoy it, too.
Eva, that's OWLMAZING!!!

We set up the carnival. The other owlets all looked SO excited! Humphrey's band played, and we all partied the night away!

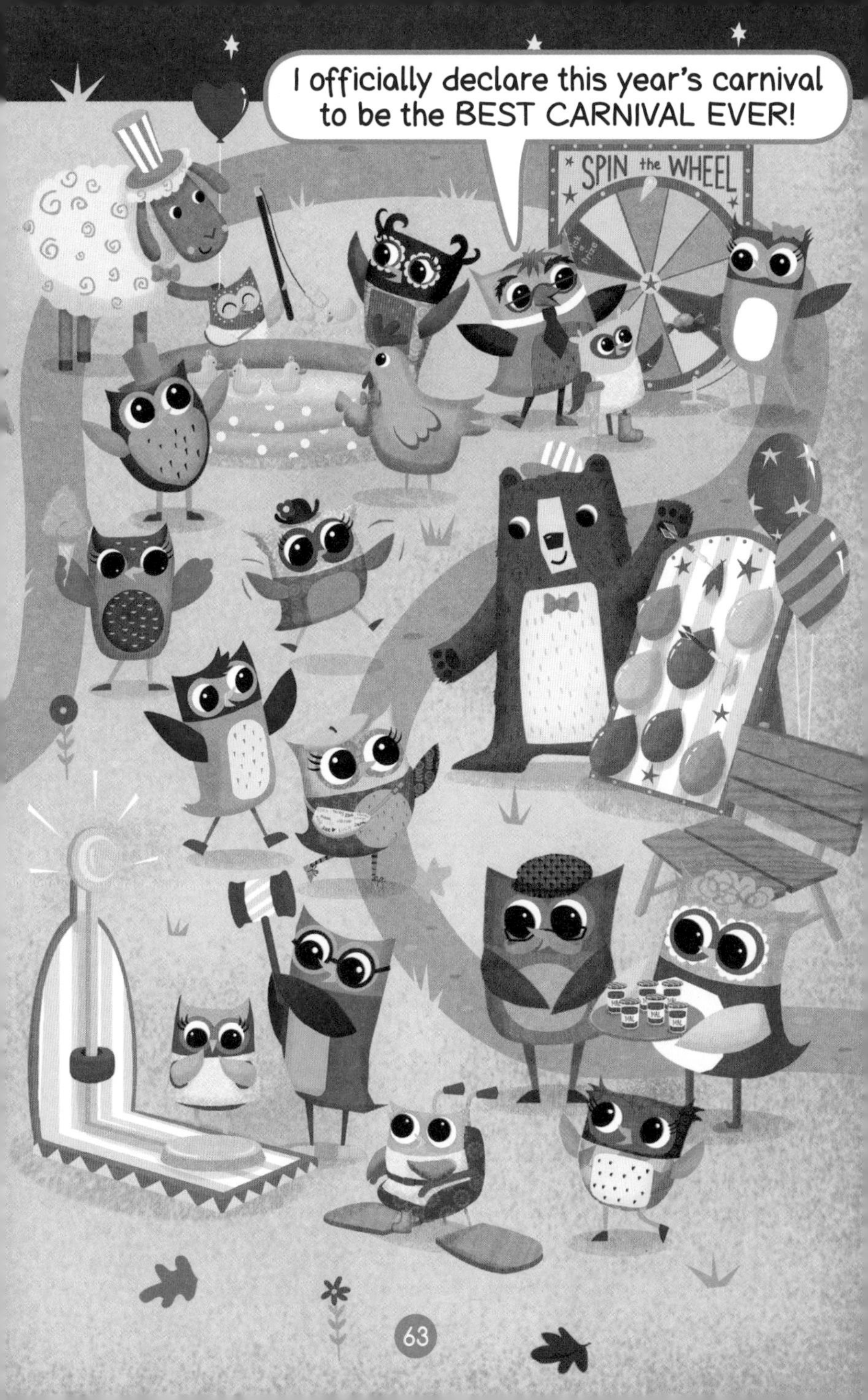
I officially declare this year's carnival to be the BEST CARNIVAL EVER!
SPIN the WHEEL

Before it was time to go home, I sat in the garden with Rocco. We watched the sun start to rise.

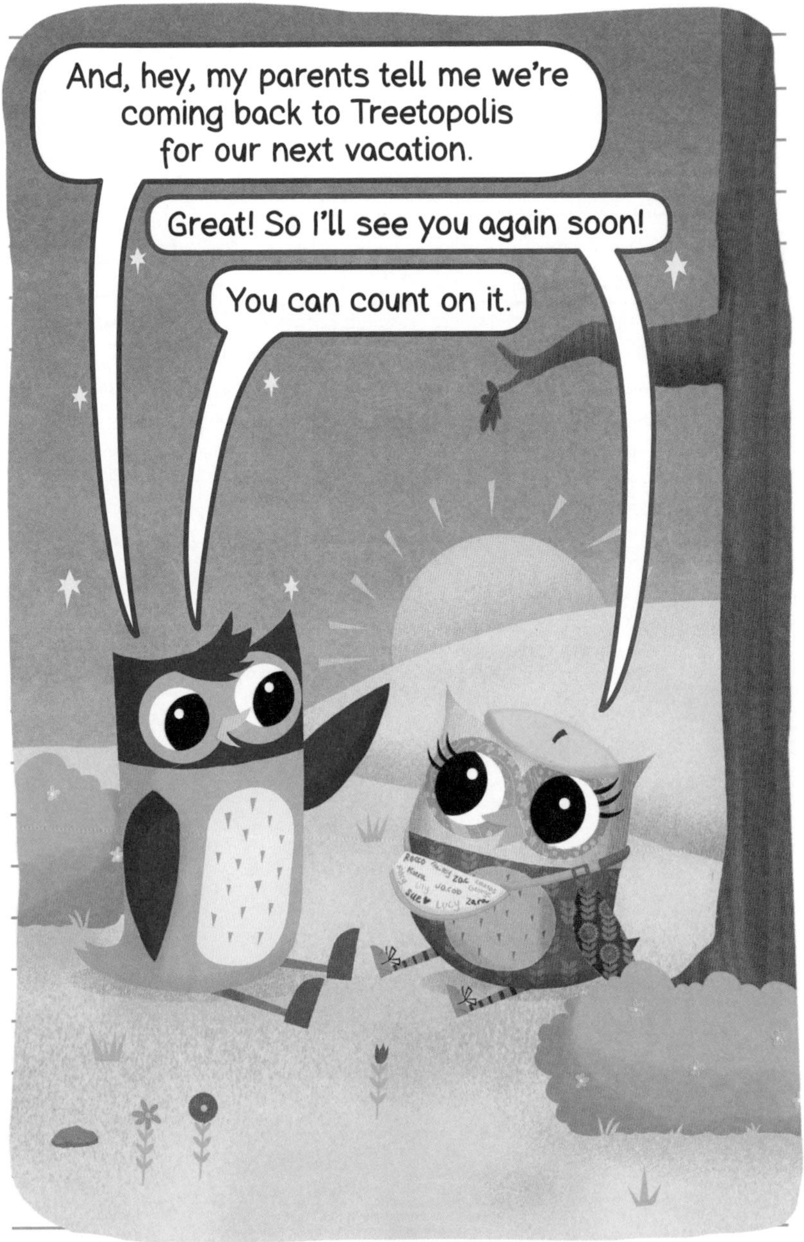
And, hey, my parents tell me we're coming back to Treetopolis for our next vacation.
Great! So I'll see you again soon!
You can count on it.

Back at home, it was time for bed.

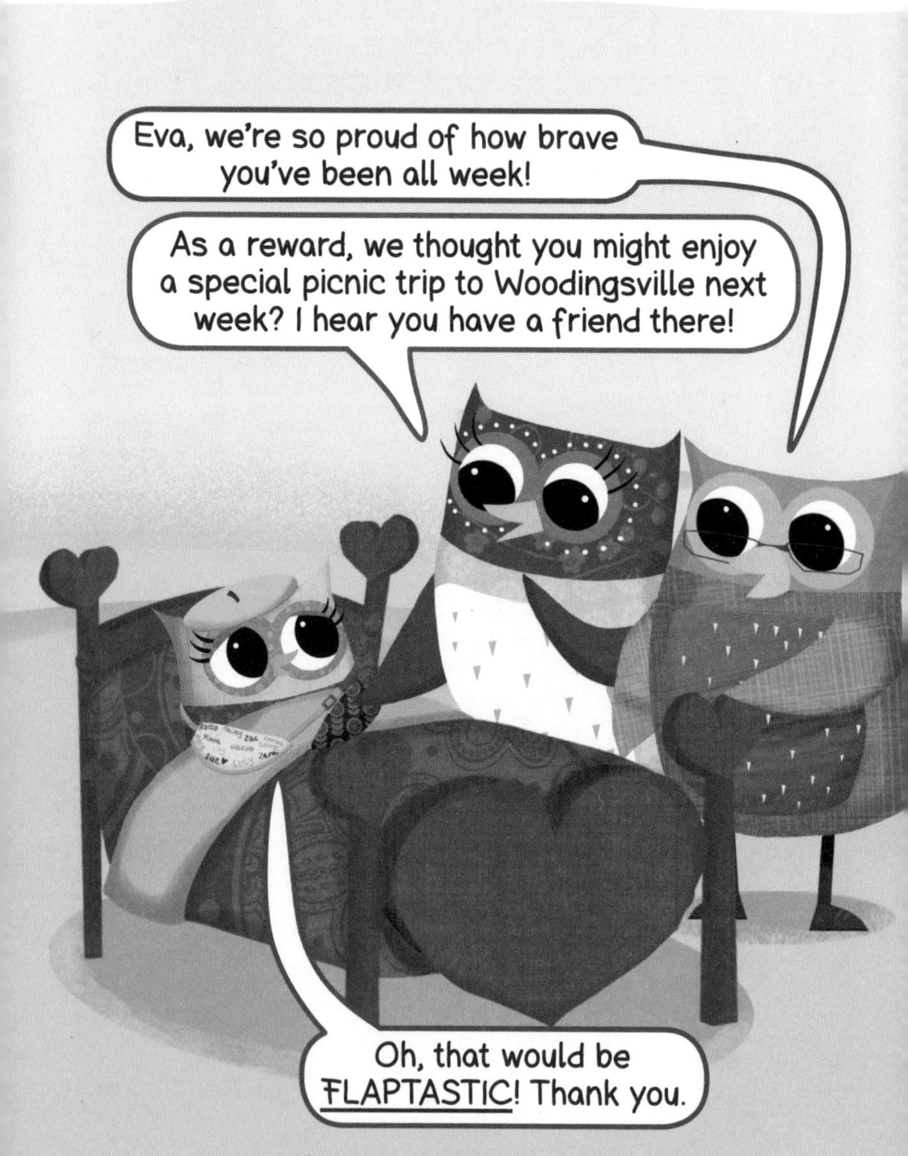
Eva, we're so proud of how brave you've been all week!
As a reward, we thought you might enjoy a special picnic trip to Woodingsville next week? I hear you have a friend there!
Oh, that would be FLAPTASTIC! Thank you.

What an amazing day, Diary! And I will get to see Rocco again REALLY soon, which is **FLAPPY-FABULOUS**! I can't wait to write and tell him the good news! I'll do it right after I get my wingsling off tomorrow! Gee, I really CANNOT wait for that to happen!

But right now, I'm super sleepy after all the fun and games.

♡ Wing-credible ♡

Saturday

Today Nurse Bobby took my wingsling off, and I finally got my wing back!

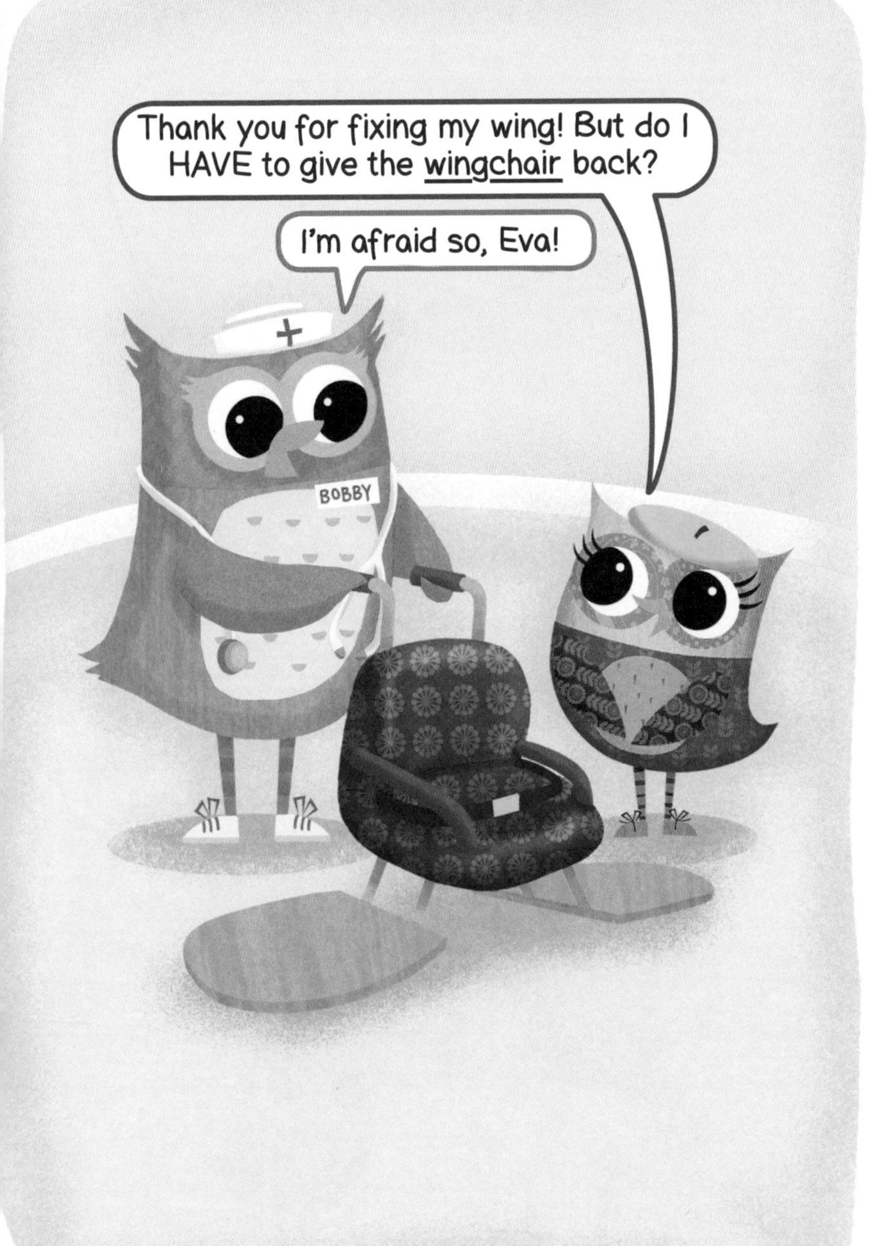
Thank you for fixing my wing! But do I HAVE to give the wingchair back?
I'm afraid so, Eva!
BOBBY

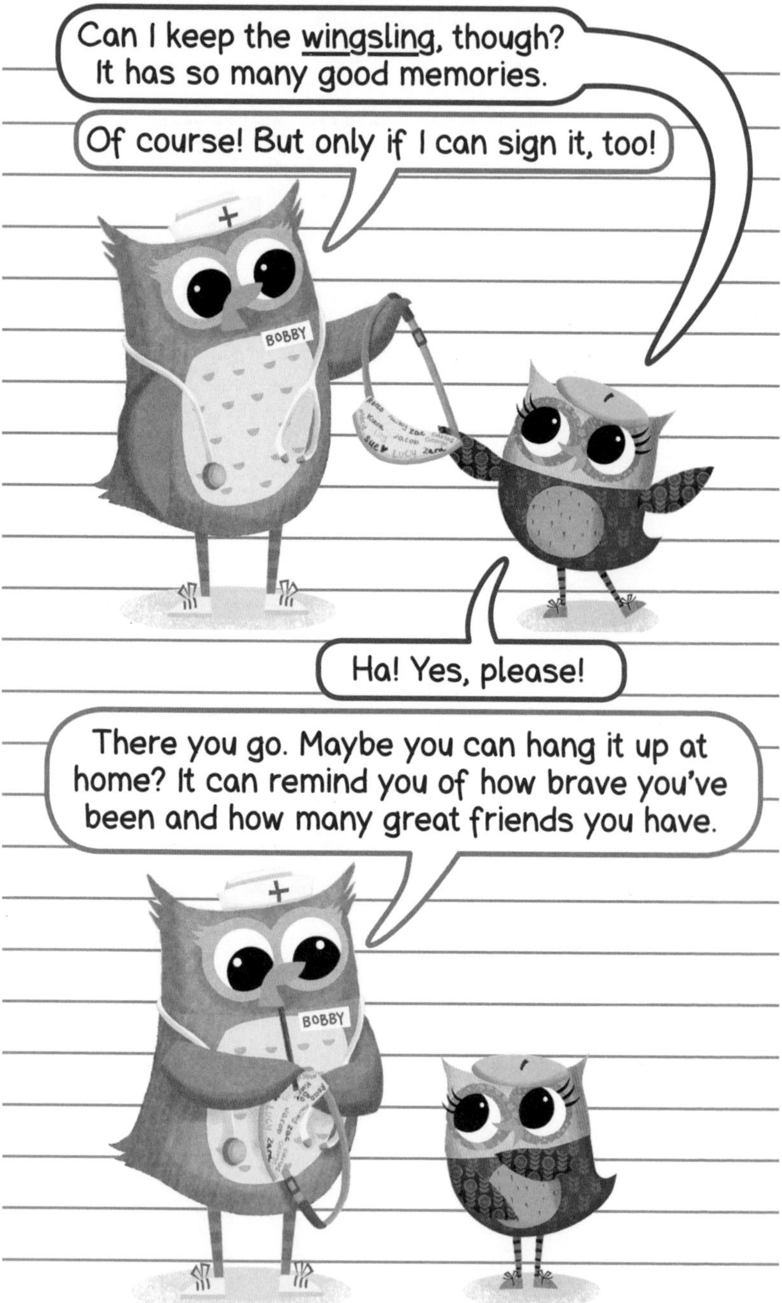
Can I keep the wingsling, though? It has so many good memories.
Of course! But only if I can sign it, too!
BOBBY
Ha! Yes, please!
There you go. Maybe you can hang it up at home? It can remind you of how brave you've been and how many great friends you have.
BOBBY

It <u>was</u> kind of sad to give the wingchair back. But I am so lucky and grateful to have two working wings again. I've really missed flying! And cuddling!

I'm also really grateful to Lucy and Humphrey for helping me write in my diary when I couldn't. Although, of course, I'll NEVER let Humphrey near my diary again!

That's what you think, Eva!!

HUMPHREY IS THE BEST BROTHER EVER. FACT.

Oh, Humphrey!!!!!

Rebecca Elliott was a lot like Eva when she was younger: She loved making things and hanging out with her best friends. Now that Rebecca is older, not much has changed — except that her best friends now include her two sons, Benjy and Toby. She still loves making things, like stories, cakes, music, and paintings. But as much as she and Eva have in common, Rebecca cannot fly or turn her head all the way around. No matter how hard she tries.

Rebecca is the author of several picture books, the young adult novel PRETTY FUNNY FOR A GIRL, and the bestselling OWL DIARIES and UNICORN DIARIES early chapter book series.

OWL DIARIES

How much do you know about Get Well, Eva?

Why can't Rocco go to the Summer Carnival? How does Eva help Rocco enjoy the carnival at the end of the story?

Reread pages 46 and 47. What happens when Eva tries to paint the carnival game? What are two words that describe how you think Eva feels in this moment?

How do Eva's friends cheer her up when she is frustrated wearing her <u>wingsling</u>? Describe a moment when you have helped a friend feel better.

Look back to the Summer Carnival artwork. Who is playing each carnival game? Which game would you most like to play?

Eva and Lucy make designs for the hat competition. What would <u>your</u> hat look like? Draw and label your hat creation!